Dear Parent:
Your child's love of reading starts here!

Every child learns to read in a different way and at his or her own speed. Some go back and forth between reading levels and read favorite books again and again. Others read through each level in order. You can help your young reader improve and become more confident by encouraging his or her own interests and abilities. From books your child reads with you to the first books he or she reads alone, there are I Can Read Books for every stage of reading:

SHARED READING
Basic language, word repetition, and whimsical illustrations, ideal for sharing with your emergent reader

BEGINNING READING
Short sentences, familiar words, and simple concepts for children eager to read on their own

READING WITH HELP
Engaging stories, longer sentences, and language play for developing readers

READING ALONE
Complex plots, challenging vocabulary, and high-interest topics for the independent reader

ADVANCED READING
Short paragraphs, chapters, and exciting themes for the perfect bridge to chapter books

I Can Read Books have introduced children to the joy of reading since 1957. Featuring award-winning authors and illustrators and a fabulous cast of beloved characters, I Can Read Books set the standard for beginning readers.

A lifetime of discovery begins with the magical words **"I Can Read!"**

Visit www.icanread.com for information on enriching your child's reading expe

MOUSE SOUP

BY ARNOLD LOBEL

HarperCollins*Publishers*

Library of Congress Cataloging-in-Publication Data

Lobel, Arnold.
  Mouse soup.
  (An I can read book)
  Summary: A mouse convinces a weasel he needs the ingredients from several stories to make a tasty mouse soup.
  [1. Mice—Fiction.] I. Title.
ISBN-10: 0-06-023967-0 (trade bdg.) — ISBN-13: 978-0-06-023967-1 (trade bdg.)
ISBN-10: 0-06-023968-9 (lib. bdg.) — ISBN-13: 978-0-06-023968-8 (lib. bdg.)
ISBN-10: 0-06-444041-9 (pbk.) — ISBN-13: 978-0-06-444041-7 (pbk.)
PZ7.L7795Mo   76-41517
[E]   CIP
                                                                                    AC

11 12 13 SCP 20 19 18 17 16 15 14 13 12
❖

THE STORIES FOR THE SOUP

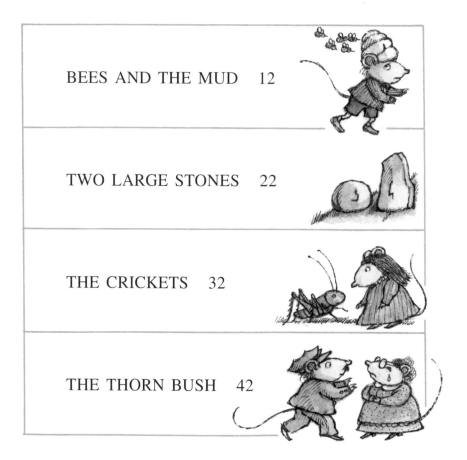

A mouse

sat under a tree.

He was reading a book.

A weasel

jumped out

and caught the mouse.

The weasel

took the mouse home.

"Ah!" said the weasel.

"I am going to make

mouse soup."

"Oh!" said the mouse.

"I am going to *be*

mouse soup."

The weasel put the mouse

in a cooking pot.

"*WAIT!*" said the mouse.

"This soup will not taste good.

It has no stories in it.

Mouse soup must be mixed

with stories

to make it taste really good."

"But I have no stories,"

said the weasel.

"I do," said the mouse.

"I can tell them now."

"All right," said the weasel.

"But hurry. I am very hungry."

"Here are four stories

to put in the soup," said the mouse.

BEES AND THE MUD

A mouse was walking

through the woods.

A nest of bees

fell from a tree.

It landed on the top of his head.

"Bees," said the mouse,

"you will have to fly away.

I do not want a nest of bees

sitting on the top

of my head."

13

But the bees said,

"We like your ears,

we like your nose,

we like your whiskers.

Oh yes, this is a fine place

for our nest.

We will never fly away."

The mouse was upset.

He did not know

what to do.

The buzzing of the bees

was very loud.

The mouse walked on.

He came to a muddy swamp.

"Bees," said the mouse,

"I have a nest like yours.

It is my home.

If you want to stay on my head,

you will have to

come home with me."

"Oh yes," said the bees.

"We like your ears,

we like your nose,

we like your whiskers.

We will be glad

to come home with you."

"Very well," said the mouse.

He stepped into the mud

up to his knees.

"Here is my front door,"

said the mouse.

"Oh yes," said the bees.

The mouse

stepped into the mud

up to his waist.

"Here is my living room,"

said the mouse.

"Oh yes," said the bees.

The mouse

stepped into the mud

up to his chin.

"Here is my bedroom,"

said the mouse.

"Oh yes," said the bees.

"And now I will go to sleep,"
said the mouse.

He ducked his head
under the mud.

"Oh no!" said the bees.

"We like your front door.

We like your living room.

We like your bedroom.

But no, no, no,

we do not like your bed!"

The bees jumped up into the air

and flew away.

The mouse went home

to take a bath.

TWO LARGE STONES

Two large stones

sat on the side of a hill.

Grass and flowers grew there.

"This side of the hill

is nice,"

said the first stone.

"But I wonder

what is on

the other side

of the hill?"

"We do not know.

We never will,"

said the second stone.

One day

a bird flew down.

"Bird, can you tell us

what is on the other side

of the hill?"

asked the stones.

The bird flew up into the sky.

He flew high over the hill.

He came back and said,

"I can see towns and castles.

I can see mountains

and valleys.

It is a wonderful sight."

The first stone said,

"All those things

are on the other side

of the hill."

"How sad,"

said the second stone.

"We cannot see them.

We never will."

The two stones

sat on the side of the hill.

They felt sad

for one hundred years.

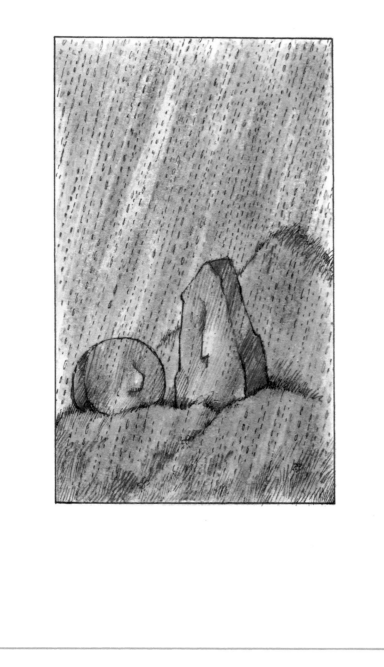

One day

a mouse walked by.

"Mouse, can you tell us

what is on the other side

of the hill?"

asked the stones.

The mouse climbed up the hill.

He put his nose over the top

and looked down.

He came back and said,

"I can see earth and stones.

I can see grass and flowers.

It is a wonderful sight."

The first stone said,

"The bird

told us a lie.

That side of the hill

looks just the same

as this side

of the hill."

"Oh good!"

said the second stone.

"We feel happy now.

We always will."

31

THE CRICKETS

One night a mouse woke up.

There was a chirping sound

outside her window.

"What is that noise?"

asked the mouse.

"What did you say?"

asked a cricket.

"I cannot hear you

and make my music

at the same time."

"I want to sleep,"
said the mouse.
"I do not want
any more music."

"What did you say?"

asked the cricket.

"You want more music?

I will find a friend."

Soon there were

two crickets chirping.

"I want you

to stop the music,"

said the mouse.

"You are giving me more!"

"What did you say?"

asked the cricket.

"You want more music?

We will find another friend."

Soon there were

three crickets chirping.

"You must stop the music,"

said the mouse.

"I am tired.

I cannot take much more!"

"What did you say?"

asked the cricket.

"You want much more music?

We will find

many friends."

Soon there were

ten crickets chirping.

"Stop!" cried the mouse.

"Your music

is too loud!"

"Loud?" asked the cricket.

"Yes, we can chirp loud."

So the ten crickets

chirped

very loud.

"Please!" shouted the mouse.

"I want to sleep.

I wish that you would all

"Go away?" asked the cricket.

"Why didn't you say so

in the first place?"

"We will go away
and chirp somewhere else,"
said the ten crickets.

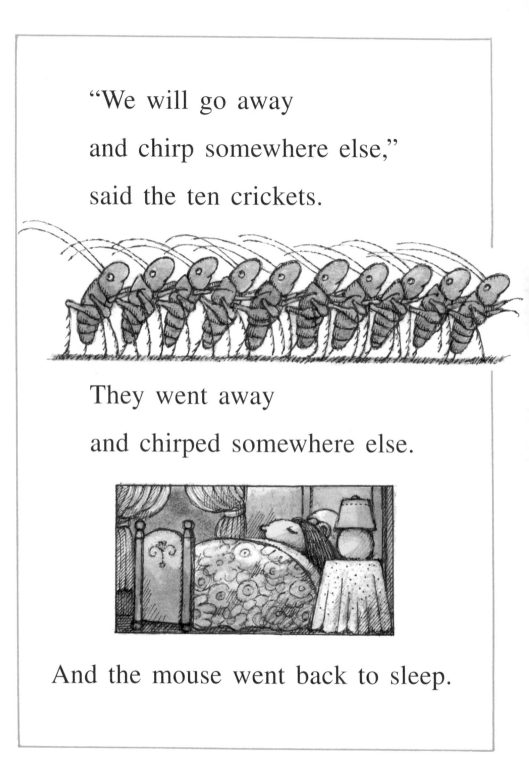

They went away
and chirped somewhere else.

And the mouse went back to sleep.

THE THORN BUSH

An old lady

went to the door

of her house.

She was crying.

A policeman came running.

"Dear lady,"

said the policeman,

"why are you crying?"

"Come in," said the old lady.

"I will show you."

"Look, there is
a thorn bush
growing in
my living-room chair,"
said the old lady.

"How did it get there?"

asked the policeman.

"I do not know,"

said the old lady.

"One day I sat down

and something hurt me.

I got up.

There was the thorn bush."

"You poor lady,"

said the policeman.

"I will pull the thorn bush

out of your chair.

Then you can sit down again."

"No!" cried the old lady.

"Don't do that!

I do not want to sit down.

I have been sitting down

all my life.

I love my thorn bush.

I am crying because it is sick.

See?" said the old lady.

"All of the branches

are falling over."

"The thorn bush
may be thirsty,"
said the policeman.
"Perhaps it needs water."
I never thought of that,"
said the old lady.
She poured some water
on the chair.

The thorn bush
shivered and shook.

Green leaves came out
on the branches.

Little buds came out
near the leaves.

The buds opened up.

They became large roses.

"Thank you, kind policeman!"

cried the old lady.

"You have saved

my thorn bush!

You have made

my house beautiful!"

She kissed the policeman

and gave him a big bunch

of roses to take home.

"There," said the mouse.

"I have told you my stories.

They will make your mouse soup

taste really good."

"All right," said the weasel,

"but how can I

put the stories into the soup?"

"That will be easy,"

said the mouse.

"Run outside and find

a nest of bees,

some mud,

two large stones,

ten crickets,

and a thorn bush.

Come back

and put them

all into the soup."

The weasel ran outside

very fast.

He forgot to close the door.

The weasel found

a nest of bees.

He was stung many times.

The weasel found

some mud.

It was wet and gooey.

The weasel found

two large stones.

They were heavy.

The weasel found

ten crickets.

He had to jump

to catch them.

The weasel found
a thorn bush.
He was pricked
and scratched.

"Now my mouse soup
will taste really good!"
said the weasel.

But when the weasel
came back to his house,
he found a surprise.
The cooking pot was empty.

The mouse hurried

to his safe home.

He lit the fire,

he ate his supper,

and he finished
reading his book.